This book belongs to:

_____

Natalie Portman's FABLES

Retellings by

NATALIE PORTMAN

Illustrations by

JANNA MATTIA

Feiwel & Friends
New York

For my favorite kids in the world,
Aleph and Amalia

A Feiwel and Friends Book

An imprint of Macmillan Publishing Group, LLC

120 Broadway, New York, NY 10271

NATALIE PORTMAN'S FABLES. Copyright © 2020 by Natalie Portman. All rights reserved.
Our books may be purchased in bulk for promotional, educational, or business use.
Please contact your local bookseller or the Macmillan Corporate and Premium Sales Department
at (800) 221-7945 ext. 5442 or by email at MacmillanSpecialMarkets@macmillan.com.
Library of Congress Control Number: 2020908579
ISBN 978-1-250-24686-8 (hardcover) — ISBN 978-1-250-80134-0 (special edition)

Book design by Mallory Grigg
Title lettering by Mike Burroughs
Printed in China by RR Donnelley Asia Printing Solutions Ltd., Dongguan City, Guangdong Province
Feiwel and Friends logo designed by Filomena Tuosto
First edition, 2020
10 9 8 7 6 5 4 3 2 1
The art was created with watercolor, gouache, and colored pencil.
mackids.com

TABLE OF CONTENTS

The Tortoise
and the Hare

Once at Sheep's vineyard, with very fine weather,
The townsimals gathered for the games together.

While sipping their juices from all types of grapes,
They cheered to find who was the greatest great ape.

But when it came time to compete with the hare,
No one stepped forward. No one would dare.

"I'm so fast and so strong, I win distance and sprint.
I'll kick up the dust, you'll just sit there and squint."

"Where's your hu-mi-li-ty?" asked Wolf that day.
"The one tea I care for is creamy Earl Grey."

Tortoise stepped forward, her home on her back.
"I'll race Mr. Hare. He's a nut I can crack.

"Hare has a sleeker and shinier sweater,
But maybe he'll learn, sometimes more isn't better."

The pig siblings gasped: "Is she brave or weak-headed?"

"*Vroom vroom*," said proud Hare, "I run fast on unleaded!"

Doe started the race with her banner all pink,
And Hare left poor Tortoise in bunny-cloud stink.

What does bunny stink smell like? I'll give you a clue.
It smells like when carrots come out in a poo.

"She's so timid, so meek, and so sheltered, so shy,
Will that weak, scaredy scampi just break down and cry?"

"What's your response to his words about you?"

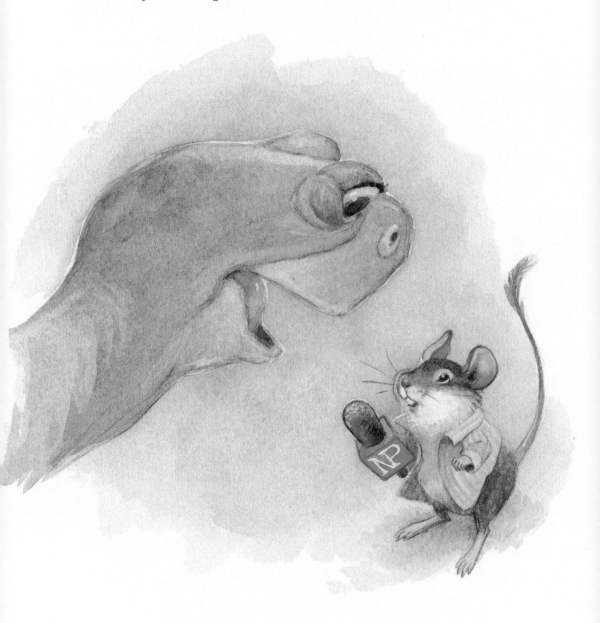

"I have nothing to say, I have too much to do."

Tortoise stayed focused on moving her feet,
Hare got distracted by drum 'n' bass beat.
"OOOOH, there's a party! I love nothing more.
There's plenty of time, I'll just dance near the door!
Then, if that slowpoke just happens on by,
I can jump out in the blink of an eye."

But Hare got sucked in by the thrum of the song,
And Tortoise, unnoticed, kept creeping along.

Tortoise drowned out the
Distraction of noise,
And plodded along with
Resilience and poise.

She knew that she didn't have
Hare's speed or sneer,
But also a braggart cannot persevere.

Tortoise took her sweet time, but enjoyed every step.
When she passed the finish line, the townsimals wept.

"We never thought a poor, burdened, old reptile
Could outpace a winner, mile after mile."

As tortoise stepped up to receive her gold
She spoke in a voice both loud and bold:

"Honey moves slowly, and it is the sweetest.
A life lived attentively is the completest."

The Three
Little Pigs

When mommy pig saw that her kids were all grown,
She told them: "It's time to move out on your own."

So Norm and Melinda and Georgie said byes,
And left their dear Mama's to build their own sties.

Norm took his couch and got takeout to eat.
He slouched on the sofa and put up his feet.

He ate noodles and noodles until he was sick,
And then his house rose from old, dirty chopsticks.

"You smell worse than me in your house made of junk,"
Said stink-master general, Norm's new squatter, Skunk.

"Do you think that chopsticks will prove to be sturdy?
I bet that they won't make it past seven thirty."

Norm sat there surrounded by cartons and boxes,
But oops! Food attracts hungry wolves and sly foxes.

"Little pig, little pig, let me come in!"
Said Wolf, as she ate out of Norm's garbage bin.

"Not by the hair of my chinny chin chin!"
Said Norm with his voice sounding terribly thin.

But Wolf was not there to be scary or mean,
She just came to say: "Even pigs should keep clean!"

Then before Norm could even begin,
Wolf huffed and she puffed and she blew his house in.

Norm left for his sister, Melinda's, new digs.
He hoped she had room for two couch-loving pigs.

Melinda loved sodas and all types of sugars.
She'd sip as she'd pick and then flick all her boogers.

As she just sat there, without even knowing,
The pile of plastic kept growing and growing.

Chimp was her nosy and noisy new neighbor,
She said, "Dear Melinda, you must learn to labor.
A house built of straws! Why, your thinking is hazy.
To have strong foundations, you cannot be lazy."

But before she could answer, Wolf knocked at her door.
Melinda was shaking; her head was aroar.

"Little pig, little pig, let me come in!"
"Not by the hair of my chinny chin chin!"

Wolf had no pity; she wore a big grin.
She huffed and she puffed and she blew her house in.

Now Norm and Melinda walked hoof after hoof
To ask to sleep under their third sibling's roof.

Young Georgie was never a pig to sit still
And preferred to perfect pioneering pig skills.

Georgie used clay to frame windows and doors,
And stone for the walls and bamboo for the floors.

Even though Georgie would make perfect bacon,
Wolf was impressed by the house they were making.

"Little pig, little pig, let me come in."
"Not by the hair of my chinny chin chin."

"I just want to tell you I like how you build.
You're thoughtful, hardworking, and wildly skilled!"

But Georgie had heard the two other pigs' stories,
And knew not to trust in Wolf's shower of glories.

"Let's meet at Sheep's orchard at quarter past eight.
We'll pick some red apples. Make sure you're not late."

But when Wolf arrived the next morning on time,
Georgie was already home making pie.

"Oh, I got there at six, you can ask Mr. Rooster,
Waking up early's an energy booster!"

"Then let's go tomorrow to Doe's new vines.
We'll pick some tomatoes. You'll show your designs."

But when Wolf arrived to pick the red fruit,
Georgie was already home making soup.

Georgie said: "Wolf, won't you get off of my lawn?
I woke up and picked my tomatoes at dawn.

"Come down the chimney, and join us to eat.
We'll have some hot soup and then something sweet."

Wolf scooted down into boiling hot water
And screamed as the water got hotter and hotter.

Wolf climbed out quickly. "Now I must confess
I know there's one pig with whom I should not mess."

"Waking up early and working much harder
Makes a pig stronger and safer and smarter.

"Planning and thinking out how to build cleanly
Makes your house sturdy
And keeps our Earth looking greenly."

Country Mouse
and City Mouse

*O*ne cold winter day, Grayson Mouse got a letter:
"Please come to the city, you'll see it's much better!"

His big cousin, Paulie, had sent him the note
Inviting him over but also to gloat.

Paulie wrote, "Grayson, your life is a yawn,
Come to my party, let's dance until dawn."

Grayson decided to go to the station
And set off by train for a little vacation.

The city was nothing like Gray's simple home.
Tall buildings, bright lights, and no green fields to roam.

Paulie Mouse lived in a snappy skyscraper,
Grayson Mouse lived in a nest made of paper.

City Mouse had a bright pink chandelier,
While Country Mouse slept under stars bright and clear.

Grayson put on his best coat and new shoes,
The cousins showed off all their very best moves.

Paulie said, "Cuz, meet my fabulous pals:
Check out my friends, the cool citymals."

"Look at my silverware, crystal, and things,
My necklaces, earrings, and so many rings.

"Oh, and try the fondue, it's so melty and Swiss.
You'll love it so much, you might give it a kiss."

Grayson thought, "Wow, she's got so much great cheese!
All I've got is field scraps, and my friends have fleas!"

But suddenly Cat strutted into the room
And fear filled the air with a sense of great doom.

Cat said, "You're eating my odds and my ends.
Now I will eat you and then all of your friends!"

"I'm out," said the peacock. "I'm not into danger."
Rhino said, "Friends? No, we're practically strangers."

The Ermine girls said: "Don't eat us, Cat, please.
We're just here for goody bags and the great cheese!"

Grayson grabbed Paulie and ran with her south,
Escaping Cat's big fishy-stinky-breath mouth.

When they got to the country and back to Gray's nest,
They finally felt they were safe and could rest.

The Country Mouse went to his cousin with grace
And used his rough paws to wipe tears from her face.

"You may have more toys,
And you may have more clothes,
But you certainly also have many more woes.

"You want to have friends who will stand by your side,
Not those who disown you to save their own hide.

"A true friend should care about how you are feeling
Not for your gowns or that thing on your ceiling."

Grayson's friends came, bringing treats that they found
From scavenging treasures that grew from the ground.

Doe brought some beans, and Sheep brought his grapes,
Pumpkins and melons were brought by the apes.

They sat on tree stumps and ate under the sky.
They watched shooting stars whiz-whizzaming on by.

They laughed with their friends until the sun rose.
They laughed until water came out of their nose.

Grayson said, "See? You don't need all that stuff."
Paulie said, "True friends are more than enough."

NOTE FROM THE AUTHOR

The one who led me to fall in love with language, with animals, and with art is my mother. She was the first to read to me, the first to teach me respect for all creatures, the first to draw with me and for me, and is the one who still plays with words to make me laugh. I am so lucky that she does that now for my children too, and that I get to enjoy the love letters that are her portraits of the children, seen here reading one of their favorite books.